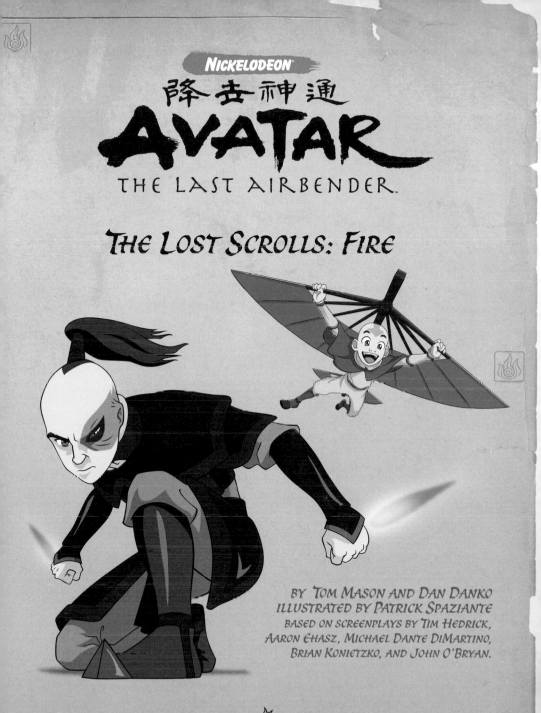

NICKELODEON

降世神通
AVATAR
THE LAST AIRBENDER

THE LOST SCROLLS: FIRE

BY TOM MASON AND DAN DANKO
ILLUSTRATED BY PATRICK SPAZIANTE
BASED ON SCREENPLAYS BY TIM HEDRICK,
AARON EHASZ, MICHAEL DANTE DIMARTINO,
BRIAN KONIETZKO, AND JOHN O'BRYAN.

SIMON SPOTLIGHT/NICKELODEON
NEW YORK   LONDON   TORONTO   SYDNEY

visit us at www.abdopublishing.com

Reinforced library bound edition published in 2008 by Spotlight, a division of ABDO Publishing Group, 8000 West 78th Street, Edina, Minnesota 55439. Published by agreement with Simon Spotlight, an imprint of Simon & Schuster Children's Publishing Division.

SIMON SPOTLIGHT

An imprint of Simon & Schuster Children's Publishing Division
1230 Avenue of the Americas, New York, NY 10020

Library of Congress Cataloging-in-Publication Data

This title was previously cataloged with the following information:

Mason, Tom.
  The lost scrolls: fire / Tom Mason ; [edited by] Sheri Tan.
    p. cm. -- (Avatar)
  I. Avatar (Television program). II. Title. III. Series.

[Fic]--dc22   2006925122

ISBN-13: 978-1-59961-458-8 (reinforced library bound edition)
ISBN-10: 1-59961-458-8 (reinforced library bound edition)

All Spotlight books have reinforced library binding
and are manufactured in the United States of America.

Prologue

3 降击神通

IF YOU ARE READING THIS,

you have uncovered one of the four hidden scrolls I have compiled about the world of Avatar. This scroll contains sacred information about the Fire Nation: stories, legends, and facts that I have found about its history and culture. I hope that this information will be as useful and intriguing to you as it is to me. In the interest of protecting the world, I ask that you keep this scroll safe, and share it only with those you trust. Beware, for there are many who wish to expose its secrets. . . .

Introduction

降去神通

Water.

Earth.

Fire.

Air.

These are the four nations of our world and the four elements that bind it together.

A few selected people of each nation possess the ability to manipulate their native element. They call themselves Waterbenders, Earthbenders, Firebenders, and Airbenders.

The most powerful bender in the world is the Avatar, the spirit of the planet incarnate. Master of all four elements, he alone maintains world order and keeps the planet balanced and peaceful.

The four nations lived together in harmony until the death of the last Avatar—Avatar Roku. Seizing the opportunity before the next Avatar—an Airbender—

could be found and trained, Fire Lord Sozin led the Fire Nation on a global campaign to wipe out the other three nations.

Only the next Avatar can stop the Fire Nation from conquering the planet, but most people believe he perished when the Fire Nation attacked the Air Nomads.

One hundred years after Avatar Roku's death, two teenage siblings have made a discovery that will forever change the destiny of the world: They have found a twelve-year-old boy frozen in an iceberg. His name is Aang, and he is the last Airbender known to be alive. He is also the world's last hope for peace and harmony.

He is . . . the Avatar.

5

The Fire Festival
LEGEND 1

"How do I look, Katara?" Aang adjusted the hand-carved Fire festival mask that covered his face. "Like everybody else," I replied. "And that's good." When traveling, the Avatar sometimes needs a disguise. I'm Katara of the Water Tribe from the South Pole. Who knew that when my brother, Sokka, and I found Aang frozen in an iceberg, he would turn out to be the Avatar? And that we'd have to help him save the world? Talk about pressure . . . and excitement!

And now we were in enemy territory, in the dreaded Fire Nation. Luckily, by wearing festival masks we could stay a little hidden.

6

I have never left the South Pole before, and I was nervous as we entered the Fire Nation village.

"I have to learn Firebending at some point, and this festival could be my only chance to watch some masters up close," Aang said as he grabbed my hand. "There's a big crowd over there. It must be good."

I wasn't so sure. A big crowd in the Fire Nation could also be bad for us.

Aang stopped in front of a stage. A Firebending magician juggled balls of fire, then waved his hands in large swirls. The fireballs turned into cooing doves that flew over the crowd.

"Thank you, ladies and gentlemen," the magician said as the crowd cheered. "For my next trick, I need a volunteer from the audience." He looked around, then pointed at me! "How about you, little lady?" he said.

I shook my head. Unfortunately, he didn't give up.

"Aw, she's shy," the magician told the audience. "Let's give her some encouragement, folks!"

The crowd applauded and gently nudged me toward the stage. I wanted to turn around and run away, but I couldn't risk calling attention to myself or to Aang, so I went onstage.

The magician tied me to a chair with a long scarf. "My next trick is called 'taming the dragon,'" he announced. I had a bad feeling about that.

His arms jerked and locked into position. I recognized the basic Firebending move. The air around me warmed as smoke swirled through his fingers.

Suddenly a flaming dragon burst from his hands, and I tried not to scream. The dragon dove at my head. I tried to pull away, but the scarf was tied too tightly. Then the dragon turned and looped around me again. His mouth was wide open, ready to take a fiery bite of me!

That's when Aang jumped onstage! Swirling his arms in the air, he summoned a ball of air that coiled in front of him. Then, with a flick of his hands, Aang shoved the air forward, toward the dragon.

The beast disintegrated into a colorful cloud of confetti that fluttered across the stage. Unfortunately the blast of air also ripped off Aang's mask. I was saved, but now we were in trouble—big trouble.

Recognizing the markings on Aang's head, someone shouted, "Hey! That kid's the Avatar!"

Sokka quickly jumped up and untied me. "It's time to go," he said. I couldn't have agreed more!

A young man also joined us. "My name is Chey," he said. "I can get you out of here!" He threw a smoke bomb onto the ground, and we took off, hidden by the thick gray cloud.

We learned that Chey was a deserter from the Fire Nation army. He led us to the camp of a legendary

Firebender named Jeong Jeong, who wanted no part of Fire Lord Sozin's war against the other nations.

Jeong Jeong's camp was at a clearing, deep in the woods. The aged Firebender was a ragged old man with long hair, a scraggly beard, and an odd-shaped battle scar. He looked like he'd been through a lot.

Aang approached him. "Master, I'm the Avatar," he said. "I need to learn Firebending."

I was shocked when Jeong Jeong refused Aang's request. He said Aang wasn't ready! "I had a pupil once who had no interest in learning discipline," Jeong Jeong explained. "Learn restraint, or you risk destroying yourself and everything you love."

But Jeong Jeong soon had a mysterious visitor—

the spirit of Avatar Roku, the previous Avatar, who ordered him to teach Firebending to Aang.

Jeong Jeong had to agree. Who could argue with an Avatar?

"Watch carefully," Jeong Jeong told Aang.

I watched Jeong Jeong pick up a dead leaf from the ground and gently wave his hand over it. The center of the leaf burst into flame. That was a better trick than the one performed by the magician from the festival! He handed the burning leaf to Aang.

"Keep this flame from reaching the edges of the leaf for as long as you can," he said before leaving Aang alone.

Aang concentrated, and the small flame smoldered in the center of the leaf.

"I did it!" Aang exclaimed. I could tell that he was impatient. These moves were simple, and Aang wanted more. He tried a Firebending move on the leaf. His right hand stiffened and pointed at the flame. It burst into the air.

"Aang, be careful," I said, worried that he was doing too much, too soon.

Aang juggled the flame, but all of a sudden he lost control. A fireball flew toward me, and I couldn't stop it!

I knelt by the river and bended the cool water

over my burning hands. In an instant the pain and redness were gone. I felt much better.

"You have healing abilities," Jeong Jeong said, smiling. "Like the great benders of the Water Tribes. Water brings healing and life; fire brings only destruction and pain."

Suddenly we heard the dull roar of boat engines coming up the river at full speed. "Zhao!" Jeong Jeong exclaimed. He had found us. The evil admiral Zhao, leader of the Fire Nation navy, must have picked up our trail at the festival. I had to warn Aang. We had to get out of there.

Jeong Jeong pulled me to my feet and pushed me toward the woods. "Get your friends, and flee. Hurry!"

When I reached camp, Aang apologized for the accident. "Jeong Jeong tried to tell me that I wasn't ready," he said, "and I wouldn't listen. I couldn't imagine what it would feel like to hurt someone like that."

I rested my hand on his shoulder. I had never seen Aang so sad. "It's all right," I said. "But we have to leave. Zhao is here, and he's captured Jeong Jeong."

Aang jumped to his feet and raced toward the river. "I have to help him!"

Zhao was waiting for us. "Let's find out what my old master has taught you, Avatar," he said with a growl.

"You were Jeong Jeong's student?" Aang asked.

"Until I got bored," Admiral Zhao replied as he thrust his arms forward. Fireballs shot from his hands toward Aang, but he dove out of the way.

Zhao was a Firebending master. I'm sure he had experiences and abilities far beyond those of Aang, but Aang had youth and energy on his side—plus he was the Avatar. I hoped that was enough.

"I see Jeong Jeong taught you how to duck and run like a coward," Admiral Zhao said, sneering. "But I doubt he showed you what a Firebender is truly capable of."

Zhao unleashed a barrage of multiple fire blasts. I felt the heat even from where I was standing. Aang raced across the edge of the water and jumped onto the deck of Admiral Zhao's ship.

"Ahoy! Look at me!" Aang taunted. "I'm Admiral Zhao!"

Zhao jumped on deck after him, hurling multiple fireballs toward Aang, blasting wildly.

"Sloppy. Very sloppy, Admiral," Aang said.

Admiral Zhao chased Aang from deck to deck, but Aang was too fast for him. Aang leaped aboard the last boat, with nowhere else to run.

"I have you now, you little smart-mouth," Zhao said smugly.

"You've lost this battle, Admiral." I couldn't believe how confident Aang was!

"Are you crazy, Avatar? You haven't thrown a single blow."

"No, but you have." Aang motioned around him. Zhao's ships were on fire. Thick, black smoke rose high into the air. "Jeong Jeong said you had

no restraint. I just got out of the way while you destroyed yourself."

Aang had won. I was so proud of him. Without using Firebending, he had defeated a more powerful enemy.

When Zhao realized what he had done, he cried out "No!" before unleashing a final fire blast at Aang. Aang flipped backward, landing on his feet in the shallow water by the riverbank. "Have a nice walk home!" he called.

Jeong Jeong and his tribe had disappeared during the battle. We couldn't find them anywhere. We were safe for now, but Zhao would no doubt track us again. Revenge is a powerful force in the Fire Nation.

The Fire Nation and Its Philosophy

The Fire Nation is mysterious and secretive. Little is known about its culture because it is difficult to infiltrate the group and gather information. No one ever leaves the Fire Nation and lives to reveal its secrets.

The leaders of the Fire Nation are driven by a single goal: to destroy all other nations and conquer the world. Not all citizens of the Fire Nation are dedicated to the cause, but they live under the oppressive rule of the Fire lord.

FIRE NATION INSIGNIA

The Fire Nation insignia is a stylized flame with three points at the top and a rounded bottom. The symbol is used primarily on flags and uniforms and to mark Fire Nation territories.

FIRE NATION FLAG

The Fire Nation flag is a triangle—shaped banner with the stylized flame insignia at its center. Six thin stripes extend from the slanted edge.

FIRE NATION LEADERS

The tyrannical Fire lord is the ultimate ruler of the Fire Nation. He is the most powerful Firebender, and his will must be obeyed. The title of Fire lord is passed down to each generation's eldest son through one family. However, the current Fire lord, Ozai, is the second—eldest son. He schemed against his father and his older brother, Iroh, to claim the throne for himself.

Fire Lord Ozai

Fire Lord Azulon

Iroh

FIRE LORD SOZIN

The architect of the war, Fire Lord Sozin
was driven by one goal: to create a world where
Fire exists as the dominant element and no nation
could challenge his rule. When Roku died, Sozin
increased his powers, drawing energy from a
passing comet. Knowing that the next Avatar
would be an Airbender, he attacked the Air
Nomads, wiping them all out (except for Aang).
Then he began to invade the Water Tribes and the
Earth Kingdom.

Fighting
the war for
decades, Sozin
died before
his dream was
realized. Now
his destructive
plan is being
carried
out by his
descendants.

FIRE LORD OZAI

The grandson of Fire Lord Sozin, Ozai is the current Fire lord. Ozai will stop at nothing in his quest for world domination. Like the Fire lords before him, he rules through fear and intimidation.

LOCATION

The Fire Nation is located on a group of volcanic islands near the equator. It is a hot, barren land, and the active volcanoes give the Fire Nation an unlimited source of power. Though based on the islands, the Fire Nation has its army and navy engaged in campaigns all over the world.

SEASON

The Fire Nation's dominant season is summer.

POWER SOURCES

Firebenders draw their energy from heat sources, most commonly the sun, but also from volcanic energy, lightning, and comets.

NATURAL RESOURCES AND FOOD

The Fire Nation has many skilled metalworkers who use iron to build the group's fortresses and warships. It powers massive furnaces with coal dug from mines by its prisoners. Its people eat rice, noodles, cabbages, and lychee nuts. They also drink plenty of tea. Having a taste for spicier fare, they also enjoy fire cakes and flaming fire flakes.

INDUSTRIES

Because the Fire Nation focuses on global conquest, it is actively engaged in building ships, manufacturing weapons (such as fire catapults, arrows and spears, swords, and knives), and shaping metal.

FIRE NATION ARMY/NAVY

   Admiral Zhao is the leader of the Fire Nation navy and Prince Zuko's nemesis. A former student of the legendary master Jeong Jeong, Zhao is a ruthless Firebender who lacks the patience to properly or strategically use his skills. That is often his downfall.

22

SHIPS

Ships in the Fire Nation are made from solid iron, to resist attacks from other nations. They are fueled by coal.

PRISONS

Fire Nation prisons are also facilities where prisoners from other nations are put to hard work. Built of sturdy metal, one such prison is a stationary shipyard in the middle of the ocean. An enormous wall bisects this structure. On one side is a shipyard, where the Fire Nation repairs and refuels its ships. The other side is a prison for captive Earthbenders. The prisoners cannot Earthbend because the metal rig is surrounded by water, and they are miles away from land. But the warden doesn't let the muscular Earthbenders go to waste: He forces them to work in the shipyard, building new ships for the Fire Nation navy to use to defeat the Earth Kingdom.

THE FIRE FESTIVAL

The fire festival is a traveling street fair in the villages and towns of the Fire Nation. Everyone wears hand-carved masks, and vendors sell a wide variety of local foods and trinkets. There are puppet shows, Firebending magicians and jugglers, fireworks, and displays of individual and group Firebending skills. The festival also visits locales in nations where other Fire Nation members live.

24

FIRE NATION MASK ART

Fire festival masks are usually hand-carved from wood and feature expressive, stylized faces similar to Kabuki theater masks.

GAMES AND AMUSEMENTS

Fire Nation snaps were invented by the Fire Nation. These are small toys made of sulfur and flint that snap when thrown onto the ground.

The tsungi horn is a musical instrument forged from metal. The curved and highly polished horn is believed to have originated in the Fire Nation and is used in traditional music of the Avatar world.

25

ANIMALS OF THE FIRE NATION

DRAGON HAWK

Dragon hawks are an essential means of communication between factions of the Fire Nation military. Like homing pigeons, these large birds carry messages in metal containers attached to their talons.

HOG MONKEY

Members of the Fire Nation use sturdy metal traps to catch hog monkeys, but they've also caught a few unsuspecting humans who hadn't been watching where they were going.

KOMODO RHINO

Komodo rhinos are large three-horned beasts with long and powerful tails. They wear armor for protection, and are used by the military for transportation.

The Art of Firebending

Firebending is an aggressive, offensive fighting force. To make up for the lack of defensive moves, a Firebender will try to overwhelm an opponent with a barrage of blows. True Firebending power comes from controlled breathing, not necessarily physical strength or size.

Firebending draws from several ancient martial arts. Each art has its own specific moves and creates different results:

Xsing Yi—Incorporates strikes from the classic "Seven Stars": hands, feet, knees, elbows, hips, shoulders, and head.

Southern Dragon Claw—Like a dragon swooping down on its prey, this form has techniques for seizing and holding that utilize the hand.

Northern Shaolin—Developed by the Shaolin monks of ancient China, this "long-fist" style emphasizes kicking over hand fighting. Kicks are extended as far as possible without compromising balance.

FIREBENDING TECHNIQUES

Firebending moves are direct and designed for victory. No other outcome is acceptable. A quick kick or a jab creates bursts of flame that thrust forward at an opponent. Whirlwind kicks generate blazing arcs of flame. Punches unleash fireballs, while spinning kicks create rings of fire. Snapping the hand or wrist creates a deadly fire-pinwheel. When several Firebenders fight together, their combined energy enables them to shoot missiles of flame that can travel long distances.

30

STRENGTHS

Firebenders are more powerful during the day and in warm climates, when they can draw on the sun for strength. A Firebender's power is at its peak near the equator during summer.

WEAKNESSES

Darkness, a solar eclipse, and a full moon can weaken a Firebender's abilities. Firebenders are also less powerful when it's raining. Because of their aggressive nature, Firebenders traditionally lack defensive moves, which can leave them vulnerable.

FIREBENDING DUELS

An *agni-kai* is traditionally fought at sunset. The Firebenders begin back-to-back, barefoot. The goal is to overpower your opponent, knock him or her to the ground, and burn him or her. Prince Zuko got his scar by fighting against his father in an *agni-kai*.

The Fire Temple
LEGEND 2

I couldn't believe what I was seeing. A large scar of charred earth cut through the forest. Sokka pointed to heavy boot tracks. "The Fire Nation did this, Aang," he said. A beautiful forest had been destroyed. It broke my heart. I'm supposed to protect nature. I'm Aang, the Avatar from the Air Nomads. Of course, I don't really know how to be the Avatar—yet. I spent the last one hundred years frozen in an iceberg!

"How could I let this happen, Katara?" I asked Sokka's sister.

Katara picked up an acorn from the ground. "These are everywhere, Aang," she said encouragingly. "Each acorn will be a tall oak tree someday. And all the birds and animals that lived here will come back."

Katara folded the acorn into my hand, and I knew she was right. The forest would return. I suddenly felt a great sense of calm.

"Hey, everyone, we've got company," Sokka pointed out.

An old man approached us and smiled at me. "Those markings on your head. Are you the Avatar?" he asked.

I nodded.

The old man sighed like a great burden had been lifted from his shoulders. "My name is Kay-ton. Our village desperately needs your help!"

In the center of the forest, Kay-fon's village had a central hall surrounded by several houses. A tall wooden fence separated the village from the trees. Many of the houses had been damaged.

"For the last few sunsets, Hei Bai, the black-and-white spirit, has attacked our village," Kay-fon said. "No one knows why."

"As the solstice approaches," he continued, "the natural world and the spirit world grow closer." He pointed at me. "Who better to resolve a crisis between the two than the Avatar himself!"

Now it really was up to me. I just wish I knew what to do!

I stood at the entrance of the village as the last sliver of light dropped behind the trees.

How do you stop a spirit from attacking a village? I had never spoken to a spirit before. I took a deep breath. "Hello, Hei Bai. This is the Avatar. I hereby ask you to please leave this village in peace!"

I didn't have long to wait. Hei Bai materialized from the woods. He was huge and angry—and he was racing toward me!

He swiped his hand across my body. I flew backward but cushioned my fall with an Airbending move that created a pillow of air underneath me. Dealing with the spirit was going to be harder than I thought.

Sokka ran up. "We'll fight him together, Aang," he said.

But I didn't want to fight the spirit. I wanted to help him, to find out why he was attacking the village.

But before I could say anything, the spirit grabbed Sokka with one of his massive claws and returned to the woods.

"Aang!" Sokka yelped.

I unfolded my staff and snapped my glider over my back. I took off after Sokka and the spirit, riding the air currents through the trees.

"Hurry, Aang!" Sokka called out, desperately thrusting out his hand.

I swooped lower. Our fingertips brushed against one another. That's when Hei Bai faded into nothing and disappeared, taking Sokka with him.

The last thing I remember was flying into a large stone statue that looked like a panda bear.

When I awoke, it was just before sunrise. My head was pounding from when I'd hit the statue.

I had failed. Not only did I *not* protect the village, but I had lost Katara's brother to the spirit beast. It would not be easy to tell her.

When I got back to the village, Katara was sitting on the ground, staring into the woods.

"Katara, I lost him." I was afraid to look her in the eyes.

She didn't respond. It was as if she couldn't see me! I looked at my hands and realized why: I was invisible! I was in the spirit world! My crash into the statue must have triggered my Avatar state and sent me there.

That's when I saw something truly incredible—a blue dragon, gliding toward me! The sunlight shimmered off its blue scales. I could hear the steady flapping of its wings. I had to get away. If it meant to harm me, I had to lead it away from Katara.

I snapped open my glider and leaped into the air. But instead of flying, I flopped to the ground. That's when I realized Airbending was not possible in the spirit world.

The dragon landed next to me. I took a step back. You can't be too careful with dragons.

The creature opened its mouth, and one of its tendrils snapped out and gently touched my hand.

I closed my eyes, and in that instant a bright, blue flash of light washed over us.

The dragon was sending me a vision of Avatar Roku's temple. That's where I had to go to talk to Avatar Roku!

When I opened my eyes, Katara threw her arms around me. I was back from the spirit world!

"Where's Sokka?" Katara asked.

"I—I don't know . . . ," I admitted—but I did have a plan to get him back.

That night I waited at the entrance to the village. I was ready this time. Hei Bai materialized from the woods and rushed toward me.

The spirit beast growled and gnashed his teeth. I reached out my hand and touched him. There was a flash of light around my fingers, and I had a vision of a panda bear.

I pulled my hand away, and the vision disappeared.

"You're the spirit of this forest!" I said, finally understanding. "You're angry because the Fire Nation burned down your home."

Hei Bai stopped growling. He was listening to me!

"When I saw the forest had burned, I too was sad," I said. "But my friend gave me hope that the forest would grow back." I pulled out the acorn that Katara had given me and placed it on the ground.

Hei Bai changed back into the panda from my vision. He folded his paw around the acorn and left.

It wasn't long before the missing villagers stumbled out of the forest. The spirit was returning them! When Sokka walked out, Katara ran up to hug her brother. "Thank you, Aang," she said. It felt good to solve the villagers' problem and bring Sokka back. I was getting used to being the Avatar . . . at least a little bit.

Now that Sokka was back, I had to focus on my next mission. "I think I found a way to contact Avatar

Roku," I told Sokka and Katara. "If I go to his temple on the winter solstice, I can speak with his spirit."

"But the solstice is tomorrow," Katara announced.

"Yeah," I said. I knew there wasn't much time, but this could be my only chance to talk to Roku. I also knew I had a bigger problem. "And his temple is in the Fire Nation."

We left right away. I thought it was too dangerous for Katara and Sokka, but they insisted on coming with me and Momo, my lemur.

"Aang! We've got trouble," Katara pointed out as we rode on Appa, my flying bison.

It didn't look good. A dozen Fire Nation navy ships stretched out ahead of us. We had reached the edge of the Fire Nation.

"We've got to run the blockade, Aang," Sokka urged.

Once they caught sight of us, the Fire Nation navy sent fireballs streaking through the sky from the ships below. Appa barrel-rolled, then dodged the blasts. I smelled the burning ashes and felt the heat against my skin. Before the Fire Nation navy could reload and launch another volley, we flew over them— and into the Fire Nation.

Avatar Roku's temple was a multitiered building that sat atop a craggy hill of jagged rocks. Molten lava surrounded it, creating a fiery moat. Flames shot into the sky.

The entry hall of the temple was dark and creepy. I felt a chill in the air, as if the place had been abandoned for years.

Five old men in hooded red robes stepped from the shadows. "I am the Great Sage, leader of the Fire Sages. We are the guardians of the temple of the Avatar."

"I am the Avatar!" I exclaimed, relieved to be among friends.

"We know," the Great Sage said, before punching a fireball directly at me.

"Run!" I yelled. I didn't know why the Fire Sages were attacking me, but I knew it wasn't wise to wait around to find out.

We came to an intersection of two hallways. "This way!" I yelled. We turned left and came face-to-face with one of the sages. I steadied myself, ready to fight.

"I am Shyu, a friend," the hooded sage said. "I know you wish to speak to Avatar Roku. I can take you to him."

Shyu punched fire at a duct in the wall. The stone

wall slid open to reveal a secret passageway, which was lit only by lava from an underground molten river.

"If this is the Avatar's temple, why did the sages attack me?" I asked.

Shyu shook his head sadly. "Once the sages were loyal only to the Avatar. When Roku died, Fire Lord Sozin forced them to follow him."

It figured that Sozin was behind this.

A stone door slid open. We stepped out into a large atrium supported by massive stone columns. Ahead of us were two huge and heavily decorated metal doors. In the middle of the doors was a row of five keyhole-like openings.

"There's the sanctuary," Shyu said. "Once you're inside, wait for the light to hit Avatar Roku's statue. Only a fully realized Avatar is powerful enough to open these doors alone. Otherwise the sages must open the doors with five simultaneous fire blasts."

Sokka studied the torch lamps that lined the walls of the atrium.

"Five fire blasts, huh?" Sokka asked, smiling. I knew then that he had an idea.

Sokka poured oil from one of the lamps into an animal-skin casing. He sealed the top with a leather strap. "This is a little trick I picked up from my father. Once

41

you light this strap . . . kaboom! Fake Firebending."

I took the homemade bombs and shoved them into the openings. Shyu shot a line of fire across the straps.

Kaboom!

Smoke shot into the atrium, filling the room. I ran to the doors. They were scorched and blackened, but they still wouldn't open! Sokka ran a finger over the blackened doors. "That blast was as strong as any Firebending I've seen."

"Sokka, you're a genius!" Katara hugged him. "It looks like your plan worked." She reached down and patted Momo's head. "All we need now is a lemur."

I was confused. The doors still weren't open. "Did the definition of genius change in the last hundred years?" I asked.

While I hid behind one of the pillars in the atrium, Shyu ushered in the other four sages.

"Come quickly!" he said. "The Avatar has entered the sanctuary! Look at the doors." Shyu pointed to the marks on the big doors.

The Great Sage turned to the others. "Open them before he contacts Avatar Roku!"

The Fire Sages shot flame into the five openings. The doors slowly slid open with a creak of protest from their ancient hinges.

Momo was on the other side.

"We've been tricked!" the Great Sage yelled. "The lemur must have crawled through the pipes!"

Momo jumped on the Great Sage. Katara

tackled one sage and knocked him into another. Sokka wrapped a cloth around the head of the last sage and tripped him.

"Now, Aang!" Shyu yelled.

I leaped over the sages and dove through the doorway, seconds before the doors slammed shut. I was inside the sanctuary!

As the sun set, the light of the winter solstice shined through a gigantic ruby set into the wall. The light slid across the floor and up the front of the statue. The time was finally here. I bowed my head and closed my eyes.

"Avatar Roku? Are you there?" I had so many things to ask him.

When I opened my eyes, I saw mist swirling around my feet. Avatar Roku was standing in front of me. Tall, lean, and muscular, he had a long, white beard and long, white hair. At last my questions would be answered!

Roku smiled. "It's good to see you, Aang," he said in a deep and powerful voice. "I have something important to tell you. One hundred years ago Fire Lord Sozin harnessed power from a passing comet and destroyed the Air Nomads. Sozin's comet will return by the end of this summer, and Fire Lord Ozai will use its power to finish what Sozin started. The Fire lord must be defeated before the comet comes."

Roku put his hand on my shoulder. "We must go our separate ways for now, Aang. A great danger awaits you outside the sanctuary doors. I can help you, but only if you're ready."

I knew my answer. "I'm ready."

Mist swirled around us. The doors opened. The Fire Sages unleashed a fury of fire at me.

But I wasn't there. In my place was Avatar Roku. I was Roku and he was me. Roku's arm swept in front of him, creating an arc of power. The Fire Sages fell like dominoes. The sages had chained Shyu, Katara, and Sokka, but the force of Roku's power broke them free.

Stone began to crumble from the ceiling as lava bubbled from the floor. Roku was destroying his home!

The sages quickly got up and fled. A mist enveloped Roku, and when it dissipated, I was in his place. Avatar Roku was gone.

Katara, Sokka, and I ran out of the temple and quickly climbed onto Appa. As he flew us to safety, the full weight of my destiny sank in. I still had questions for Roku, but first I had to defeat the Fire lord. I had to restore balance.

I had to save the world.

The Five Fire Sages and the Spirit World

THE FIVE FIRE SAGES

The Fire Sages are the last of their kind—remnants of a bygone era in the Fire Nation when greater importance was placed on spiritual matters. They live at Avatar Roku's Fire temple on Crescent Island. Wise leaders as well as powerful Firebenders, the sages watch over the sanctuary, protect it from

46

invaders, and gather what knowledge they can about the Avatar.

The history of the sages goes back thousands of years. A council of sages led the Fire Nation in its early years. The lead sage was known as the Fire lord because of his high level of Firebending ability and his deep spiritual connection to fire. Throughout the years, the Fire lord severed ties with the sages and took over control of the Fire Nation for himself.

Now led by the Great Sage, the sages are relegated to spiritual matters only. Tensions between the Fire lord and the sages have increased with each generation.

During Fire Lord Sozin's reign, the sages remained loyal to Avatar Roku. They kept watch over the sanctuary in Roku's absence. But after the Avatar's death, Fire Lord Sozin forced them to serve only him. Now, after three generations, the sages willingly serve the Fire lord and council him on spiritual matters—except one sage, Shyu.

At age sixty, Shyu is the youngest of the Fire Sages and the only one still loyal to the Avatar. His ancestors were all sages. His grandfather was the sage who first declared—against popular belief—that the Avatar survived the Fire Nation attack on the Air temple. Many years later Shyu's father also made the determination that the Avatar was an Airbender and still alive. This was not what the Fire lord wanted to hear. Shyu's father was branded a traitor and sent away, leaving Shyu to be raised by the other sages.

Shyu is the last of his proud lineage, a sage who does not blindly follow the Fire lord. But he knows the price he would pay if he spoke out against the Fire Lord. Fire Lord Ozai has set forth a decree that anyone who helps the Avatar will be considered a traitor to the Fire Nation, and punished.

CRESCENT ISLAND

Located inside the Fire Nation, Crescent Island is home to the Fire temple of Avatar Roku. Crescent Island is a volcanic island, and its rocky landscape is crisscrossed with rivers of lava, including one that runs under the temple.

HEI BAI

Hei Bai is the black—and—white spirit who has guarded Senlin's forest for thousands of years. His natural form is a gentle panda bear, but, angered by the Fire Nation's destruction of his forest, he has changed into a snarling monster who threatens the local villagers.

THE SPIRIT WORLD

The spirit world is inhabited by a wide variety of spirit creatures who act as guardians of the rivers, forests, and mountains. The spirits of the previous Avatars are alive within the spirit world, and they watch over Aang. He may contact them during a solstice or when he enters the spirit world.

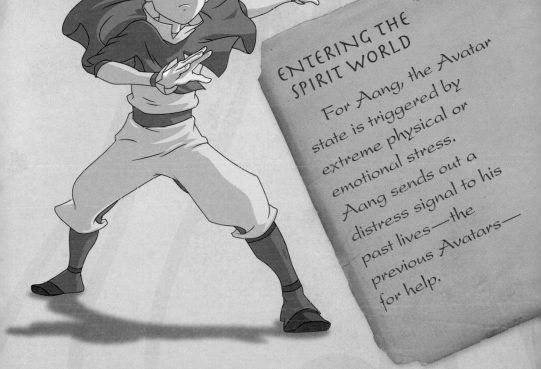

ENTERING THE SPIRIT WORLD

For Aang, the Avatar state is triggered by extreme physical or emotional stress. Aang sends out a distress signal to his past lives—the previous Avatars—for help.

RULES OF THE SPIRIT WORLD

When the bender is in the spirit world, he can still observe the natural world, but no one can see or hear him. If something bad happens to his body in the natural world, or if his body is moved, his spirit might not find its way back.

BENDING IN THE SPIRIT WORLD

Once they enter the spirit world, benders no longer have their bending ability. Because the spirit world has no physical form, a bender cannot manipulate any of the four elements.

The final tale is recounted by Prince Zuko, who once saved the Avatar's life.

The Blue Spirit
LEGEND 3

I pulled the hand-carved wooden mask over my face. I wrapped my cloak around my body to shield me in the night. No longer was I, Prince Zuko, the disgraced son of Fire Lord Ozai. I was now the Blue Spirit, and my mission was to free the Avatar.

When I heard that Admiral Zhao had captured the Avatar, I had to come up with a plan. I needed Aang to reclaim my status in the Fire Nation. I couldn't let Zhao have him.

Sneaking into the stronghold where the Avatar was held prisoner was easy. Admiral Zhao's self-congratulatory speech distracted the guards, and I slipped inside the gates.

"We are the sons and daughters of Fire," Admiral Zhao bellowed from the balcony of the Fire Nation fortress. "Only one thing stood in our path to victory: the Avatar. I am here to tell you that he is now my prisoner!"

The soldiers chanted and clanged their weapons together in response.

I removed a loose grate in the ground and disappeared into the sewer pipes under the fortress.

When I unlocked the cell door, I saw the Avatar chained between two stone columns. Fire urns burned atop each one.

Aang gasped. "Who are you?"

He had no idea! I couldn't speak or the Avatar would recognize my voice, but my disguise was perfect. I drew two broadswords and swung them through the air. Moments later Aang's chains lay at his feet. He was free. This was easier than I had imagined.

"Are you here to rescue me?" Aang asked.

I didn't respond. I opened the door and signaled for him to follow me. I couldn't believe it—I was telling the Avatar what to do!

We scampered unnoticed across the courtyard. Then suddenly a bright light cut through the darkness and fell upon our backs.

"There!" A voice cried out. We had been discovered! I couldn't let myself be captured. Zhao wouldn't understand, and neither would my father.

I drew my swords, then pointed to the open gate on the other side of the courtyard. The Avatar and I both charged toward the gate, but our escape was blocked by dozens of spearmen.

"Stay close to me," the Avatar said.

As he circled his hands, a vortex sucked the air

around him into a spiral. Then he thrust out his arms, which caused a blast of wind to plow into the soldiers, blowing them backward like leaves in a storm.

I almost laughed. I had rescued the Avatar, and now he was rescuing me. If only he knew! We rushed through the newly formed human alley. But the gate had now closed, and the troops surrounded us on all sides. We were trapped.

"Hold your fire!" Zhao called out. He pushed through the soldiers and pointed at the Avatar. "He must be captured alive!"

How could I escape with the Avatar? I had to think fast. Using his body as my shield, and grasping my swords firmly, I inched us toward the gate.

The Avatar was shocked and scared. I felt his body tremble. The Firebenders parted as Zhao stepped forward. He looked me right in the eye—and didn't recognize me!

"Open the gate," Zhao ordered. "Now."

The gates opened, and I quickly backed out of the fortress, holding the Avatar as my hostage.

Outside the gate I retreated cautiously, still hiding behind the Avatar. The outlying woods were only a few feet away. We could make it.

I never saw the arrow. I never heard it zip through the air. But I definitely felt it hit my mask with a sharp clang, and I fell to the ground.

"Prince Zuko?"

I awoke to the sound of my name. I was looking straight up at the sky through a thick canopy of trees. Dull pain ached through my body.

The Avatar sat a few feet from me, scuffed and dirty. "Why did you disguise yourself as the Blue Spirit to rescue me?"

I did not answer. I wasn't trying to rescue him. I was only taking him from Zhao in order to turn him over to my father. I tried to rise, but I couldn't. I hurt too much.

"You know, a hundred years ago, before this war started, I had plenty of friends in the Fire Nation," the Avatar said. "If we had known each other back then, do you think we could have been friends too?"

I punched a fire blast at the Avatar, trying to get the drop on him. I missed. And by the time I got to my feet, he was long gone. I thought about his question. Maybe we could have been friends once, but it's too late for that now.

I tracked the Avatar to the North Pole, to the Water Tribe. No one can hide from the son of the Fire lord. I was going to get the Avatar back. I had to.

Uncle Iroh helped me strap on the last piece of my heavy, white uniform. It was bitter cold, and the temperature was dropping fast.

"So tell me, Prince Zuko, what do you intend to do once you have the Avatar?" Iroh asked.

"Take him home to my father, of course," I said. "I shall restore my honor and reclaim my rightful place as the future ruler of the Fire Nation."

I said good-bye one last time and slid into my small boat. Chunks of ice bobbed gently on the calm surface as I paddled through the icy waters that surrounded the Water Tribe's city.

A herd of seals barked and scooted across an icy ledge and dove into the freezing water. I waited, but they did not return. I knew they must be coming up for air somewhere under the ice. But where? There was only one way to find out.

I took several deep, sharp breaths. Slivers of fire

warmed my body. Clenching my teeth, I plunged into the water, then followed the seals through an opening in the ice. When I came to the surface, I was in an underground cavern. I grabbed an icy shelf and pulled myself out of the water.

I twisted my body and exhaled in a Firebending move that instantly dried me. My body temperature was soon back to normal.

Pushing past the barking seals, I came upon a waterfall cascading from the ceiling, splashing crystal-clear water into a deep pool. That was the way out! I stepped into the waterfall, bracing against the icy water that pounded my head and body.

My hands gripped one wet, frozen rock after another. The ice was hard and densely packed. The water was numbing, but I wasn't going to stop. I melted a hole in the frozen earth and crawled through.

I was inside the city, behind enemy lines. All I had to do now was find the Avatar.

The Avatar sat cross-legged in the grass of the Water Tribe's oasis. This was the center of all spiritual energy for the Water Tribe. It was a large clearing under the surface of the North Pole, filled with flowers; thick, green grass; lush forests; and warm air. Canals crisscrossed the oasis, providing it with necessary water.

The Avatar's tattoos glowed. He was in the Avatar state and had crossed into the spirit world. Katara was by his side, looking as if she would protect him.

I stepped out from the shadows. "Well, aren't you a big girl now?" I said.

Katara spun around to face me. "Prince Zuko?"

"Yes. Hand over the Avatar, and I won't hurt you." I moved toward him, but she thrust her arms at me. The ice buckled, and I fell to the ground.

"I see you've learned a new trick," I said. "But I didn't come this far to lose to you." She couldn't take me. I had more experience, and I had fire.

I unleashed a flurry of kicks and punches. Katara backed away but repeatedly blocked my blows with ice beams. I soon realized I was surrounded by them.

I shattered the beams with swift fire kicks. "You've found a master, haven't you?"

She was good, but I was not going to let her beat me. I charged at her with my fire daggers. But she created a thick layer of ice around my face so I couldn't see!

All of a sudden a sharp piece of ice knocked me across the oasis. I fell into the canal. Then, with a determined wave of her arms, she froze the canal, hoping to hold me in place. No chance. I broke free, but she produced a water cannon. The blast tossed me farther down the canal!

She was good, but I couldn't let her win. As I lay on my back, I looked up to the sky. Night was over—the sun was rising.

I took a deep breath and felt the power of the sunlight surge through my body. With a strong Firebending blast, I made Katara fly backward into a wall, and she fell to the ground.

"You rise with the moon," I said. "I rise with the sun." I had won. The Avatar was finally mine.

Yes, I finally had the Avatar in my possession. But the blizzard outside was preventing me from taking him to my father.

The driving snow and icy winds that night forced me to seek shelter in a cave. The Avatar was still in his meditative state. His eyes were closed, but his tattoos glowed, pulsing slowly and regularly. I don't know where his spirit was, and I didn't care. I had the Avatar's body. That was all I needed to show my father. That was all I needed to regain my honor.

A bright light burst into the cave and enveloped the Avatar. His spirit had returned. His eyes flickered awake. "Welcome back," I said sarcastically.

"Good to be back," the Avatar replied.

He tried to get up, but immediately fell on his face. I had tied him from head to toe. I could not risk him using his Airbending abilities against me.

My joy was short-lived, though. Soon his flying

bison landed outside the cave, bringing Katara with him. They must have tracked the Avatar's spirit!

"Here for a rematch?" I asked.

"It's a full moon, Zuko. It's not going to be much of a match."

She was right. I had forgotten about the moon. The Water Tribe draws tremendous power from the night, and a full moon makes them even stronger.

The girl unleashed a furious Waterbending move, one I had not seen before. I hurried to block it, but it was too much for me. Frozen in place, I slid backward and crashed against the side of the cave. I had lost the Avatar . . . again!

But there would be other battles to fight, other chances to catch the Avatar and restore my honor. My quest was definitely far from over.

This is what I know from stories passed along to me.

PRINCE ZUKO

The eldest son of Fire Lord Ozai, Prince Zuko is the rightful heir to the Fire lord's throne. But the passionate Firebender was banished from the Fire Nation when he spoke out against his father and the war.

The only way Prince Zuko can return home and restore his birthright and honor is to find the Avatar and present him to his father.

Accompanying him is his uncle Iroh, Fire Lord Ozai's older brother.

Zuko possesses great Firebending skills. He's very persistent and never gives up. Unfortunately he's also arrogant and impatient, weaknesses that can hurt his quest to capture the Avatar.

UNCLE IROH

General Iroh is Lord Ozai's older brother and Prince Zuko's uncle. Before he retired, his army led a siege on Ba Sing Se, the great Earth Kingdom capital for six hundred days. After losing countless men in the siege, and with no end to the battle in sight, General Iroh ordered his men to retreat, an act deemed cowardly by Fire Lord Ozai.

Iroh is responsible for perfecting Zuko's Firebending skills. He is protective of Prince Zuko and tries to get him to learn self-control and make more careful decisions.

Epilogue

IT TOOK A HUNDRED YEARS OF WAITING,

but the new Avatar has arrived . . . in the body of a twelve-year-old boy. Though the Air Nomads have ceased to exist, their spirit lives within Aang, the Avatar and the last Airbender. The Water Tribes have defeated the Fire lord for now, but he will doubtlessly return. The Earth Kingdom is also under constant threat.

As I conclude and seal this scroll, the Fire Nation is regrouping, and Aang is on his way to mastering the other elements. He must defeat the Fire Lord before Sozin's comet returns to give Ozai its unlimited power. This is all I know so far. Please do not show this scroll to anyone whose trustworthiness you doubt. The fate of the world is in your hands!

降去神通